THE FABLE OF THE FIG TREE

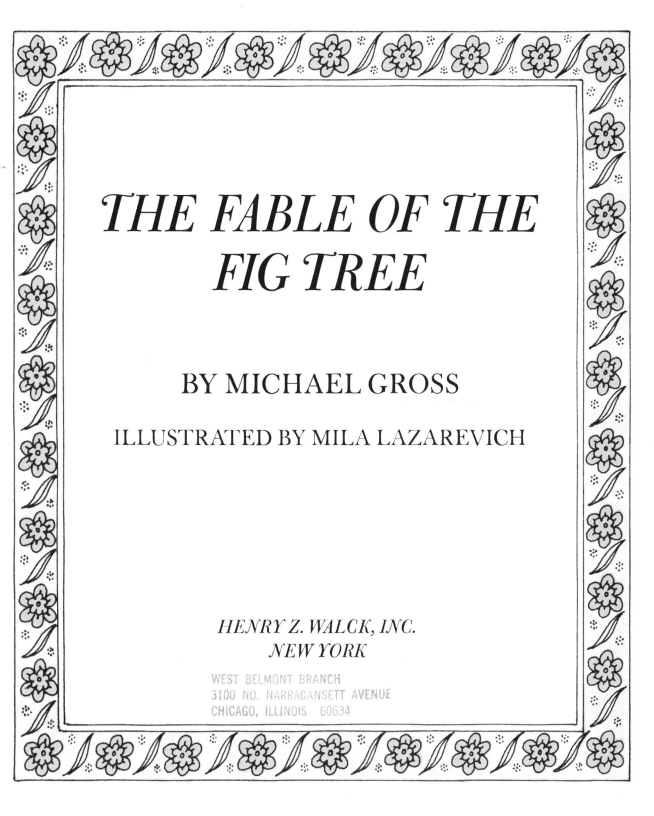

THE FABLE OF THE FIG TREE

BY MICHAEL GROSS

ILLUSTRATED BY MILA LAZAREVICH

HENRY Z. WALCK, INC.
NEW YORK

Text copyright © 1975 by Michael Gross
Illustrations copyright © 1975 by Mila Lazarevich
ISBN: 0-8098-1228-2
LC: 74-25972
Printed in the United States of America

Library of Congress Cataloging in Publication Data
Gross, Michael.
    The fable of the fig tree.
    SUMMARY: When he hears how his neighbor was rewarded
by the king, a greedy man tries to get a reward the
same way.
    [1. Folklore, Jewish]   I. Lazarevich, Mila, ill.
II. Title.
PZ8.1.G89Fab   398.2'2   [E]   74-25972
ISBN 0-8098-1228-2

For my two youngest grandchildren
Elizabeth and Peter

In an ancient and tiny kingdom, in what is now called Turkey, there once ruled a king who was known throughout the land for his wisdom, his goodness and his loving kindness.

Now it so happened that one bright and sunny morning the king strolled through the little village that nestled snugly in the shadow of the palace. There he came across an old man planting a small fig tree in front of his cottage, and the king stopped to admire the skill with which the old man worked.

"Tell me," the king said, as the man straightened up from his labor, "how old are you?"

"I am in my eighty-second year," the man, Elisha, replied.

"And how long will it be before this tree you are planting will bear fruit?" was the king's next question.

"Five years," the man answered.

The king thought for a moment. "You are now past eighty, and it will be five years before the tree bears fruit. How can you be sure that you will live long enough to eat the figs it will bear?"

Elisha said, "If the Lord desires it, I hope to do so. If not, my children will gather the fruit. My parents, and their parents before them, and all the generations of parents before them, planted trees for their children. Thus it is my duty to plant trees for my children."

The answer gave the king much pleasure and he embraced the old man, saying, "May God bless you for many more years. If it so happens that when the figs ripen, you are here to gather them, bring me some. I will enjoy the fruit all the more from having seen the tree planted from which it grew."

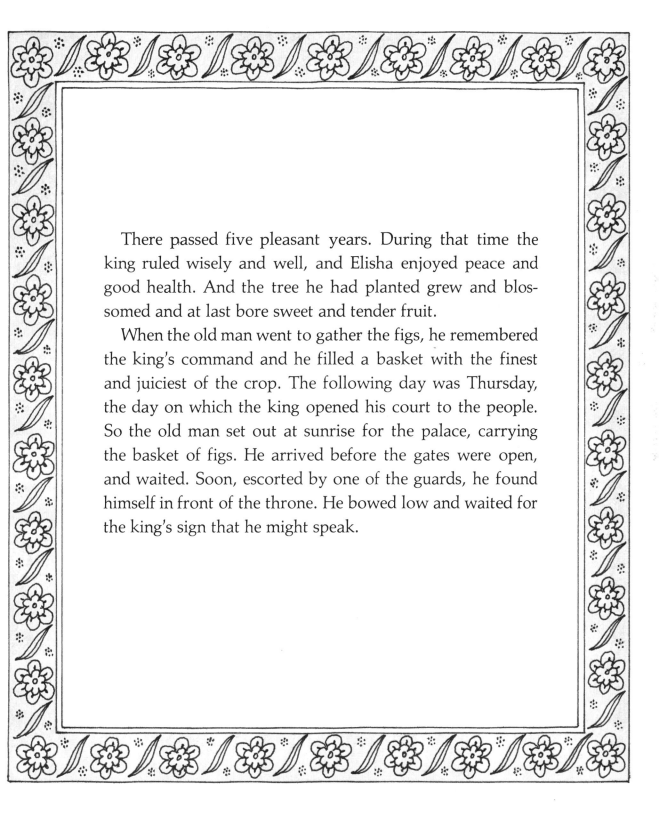

There passed five pleasant years. During that time the king ruled wisely and well, and Elisha enjoyed peace and good health. And the tree he had planted grew and blossomed and at last bore sweet and tender fruit.

When the old man went to gather the figs, he remembered the king's command and he filled a basket with the finest and juiciest of the crop. The following day was Thursday, the day on which the king opened his court to the people. So the old man set out at sunrise for the palace, carrying the basket of figs. He arrived before the gates were open, and waited. Soon, escorted by one of the guards, he found himself in front of the throne. He bowed low and waited for the king's sign that he might speak.

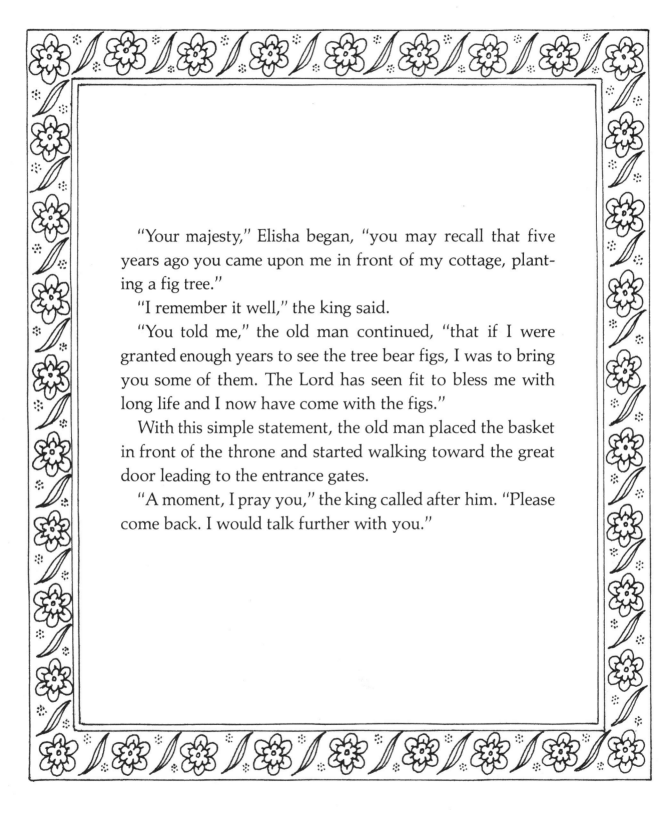

"Your majesty," Elisha began, "you may recall that five years ago you came upon me in front of my cottage, planting a fig tree."

"I remember it well," the king said.

"You told me," the old man continued, "that if I were granted enough years to see the tree bear figs, I was to bring you some of them. The Lord has seen fit to bless me with long life and I now have come with the figs."

With this simple statement, the old man placed the basket in front of the throne and started walking toward the great door leading to the entrance gates.

"A moment, I pray you," the king called after him. "Please come back. I would talk further with you."

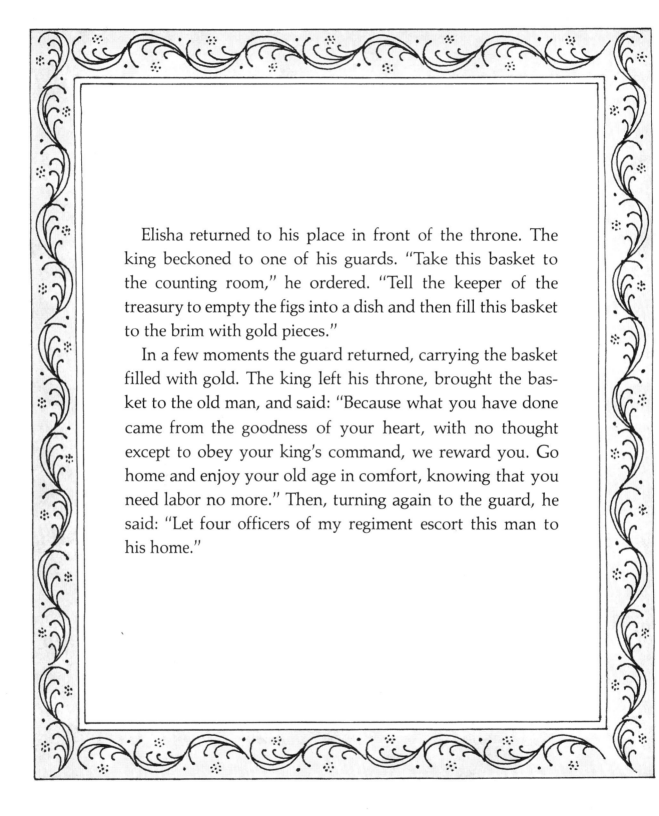

Elisha returned to his place in front of the throne. The king beckoned to one of his guards. "Take this basket to the counting room," he ordered. "Tell the keeper of the treasury to empty the figs into a dish and then fill this basket to the brim with gold pieces."

In a few moments the guard returned, carrying the basket filled with gold. The king left his throne, brought the basket to the old man, and said: "Because what you have done came from the goodness of your heart, with no thought except to obey your king's command, we reward you. Go home and enjoy your old age in comfort, knowing that you need labor no more." Then, turning again to the guard, he said: "Let four officers of my regiment escort this man to his home."

So the officers, with great ceremony, escorted the old man back to the square of the little village from which he had come. The neighbors, astonished at seeing one of their

humblest citizens being paid such honor, flocked to the square. They watched silently until the officers saluted and marched away.

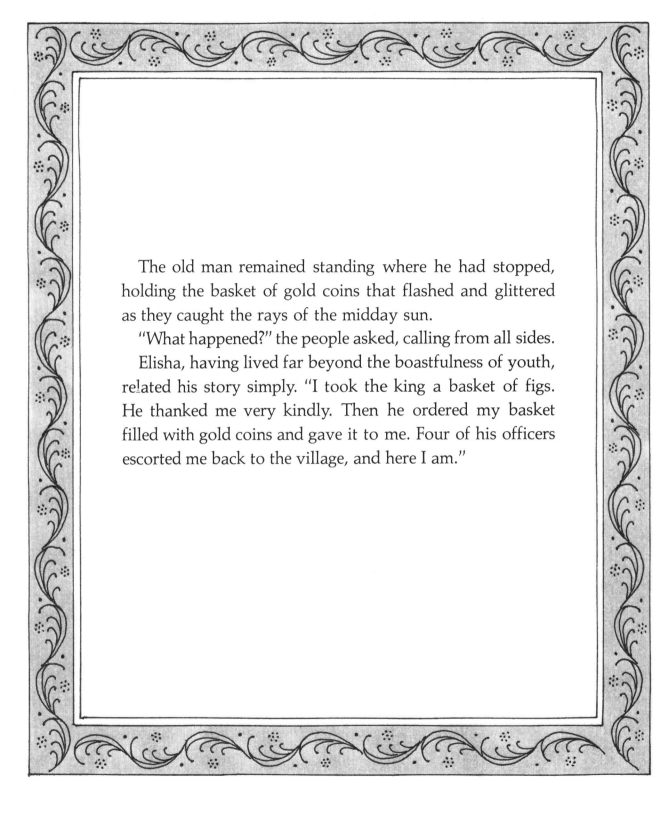

The old man remained standing where he had stopped, holding the basket of gold coins that flashed and glittered as they caught the rays of the midday sun.

"What happened?" the people asked, calling from all sides.

Elisha, having lived far beyond the boastfulness of youth, related his story simply. "I took the king a basket of figs. He thanked me very kindly. Then he ordered my basket filled with gold coins and gave it to me. Four of his officers escorted me back to the village, and here I am."

All the villagers joined in congratulating the old man on his good fortune and joyously drank to his health and long life, emptying the dozen bottles of sparkling wine that one of the gold pieces had bought.

But, as has always happened, and will continue to happen just as long as this world continues to spin, there was one villager who envied the old man his good luck. And the envy burned within him and gave him no peace.

That night, while the wife of this wretched man was preparing the evening meal, he could contain himself no longer. "Did you hear of the astounding thing that happened to Elisha the farmer?" he asked her.

"I have been in the house all day," his wife answered, "and no one has come to visit. What happened?"

"It seems the old man got a sudden notion to take a basket of figs to the castle. The king himself accepted the gift, and filled the old man's basket full of gold pieces. He gave the basket to the old man and sent four soldiers to see that he got safely home. Isn't that the strangest thing you have ever heard?"

"It is indeed a surprising thing," his wife agreed.

"I would be a fool not to profit by this happening," her husband said. "Next Thursday, when the king again opens his court, I will bring him a load of figs in the biggest basket we have. When he fills that up with gold, we'll have enough money to buy this cottage and live in riches for the rest of our lives."

And so, early the following Thursday, this greedy creature searched out the largest basket he could find, loaded it to the top with whatever figs he could lay his hands on, good or bad, and set off for the palace.

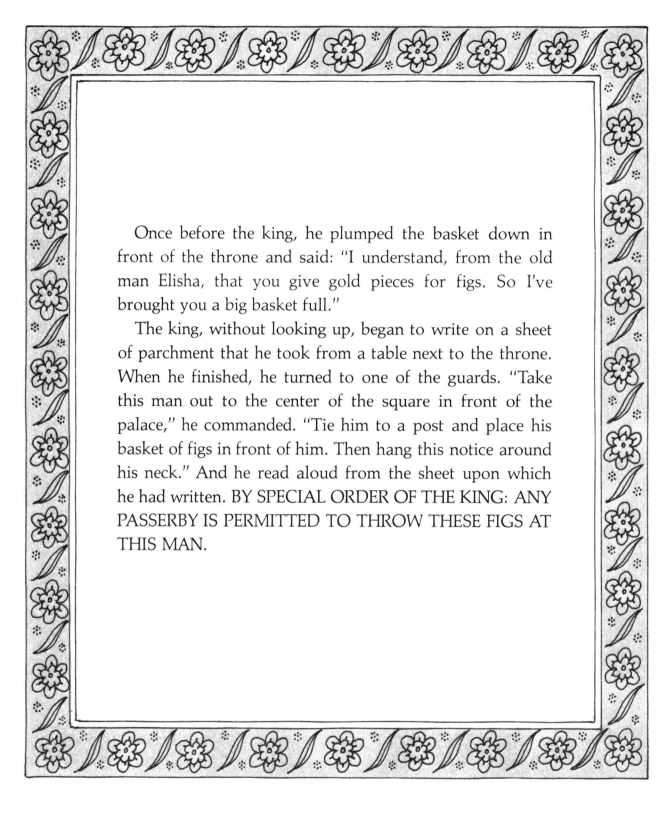

Once before the king, he plumped the basket down in front of the throne and said: "I understand, from the old man Elisha, that you give gold pieces for figs. So I've brought you a big basket full."

The king, without looking up, began to write on a sheet of parchment that he took from a table next to the throne. When he finished, he turned to one of the guards. "Take this man out to the center of the square in front of the palace," he commanded. "Tie him to a post and place his basket of figs in front of him. Then hang this notice around his neck." And he read aloud from the sheet upon which he had written. BY SPECIAL ORDER OF THE KING: ANY PASSERBY IS PERMITTED TO THROW THESE FIGS AT THIS MAN.

So, all during that long, hot afternoon, the greedy man was pelted with the hundreds of figs he had brought, until

every last one had been thrown. Then the guards untied him and hustled him onto the highway, flinging the empty basket after him.

The sun had just disappeared when this woeful wreck of a man entered his home. His nose was bloody, one of his eyes had been blackened, his hair was full of fig juice, and his clothing hung about him in shreds.

"What in heaven's name has happened to you?" his wife cried, throwing up her hands in horror.

Her husband told her of the misery and pain he had gone through, but his wife remained silent.

"Why are you so quiet?" he finally asked.

His wife thought a little longer, then she spoke, "I think you ought to thank the Lord you took a basket of figs. Suppose, instead, you had taken hazelnuts. With figs it hasn't been too bad."

And while her husband washed and put on fresh clothing, the woman prepared their dinner.